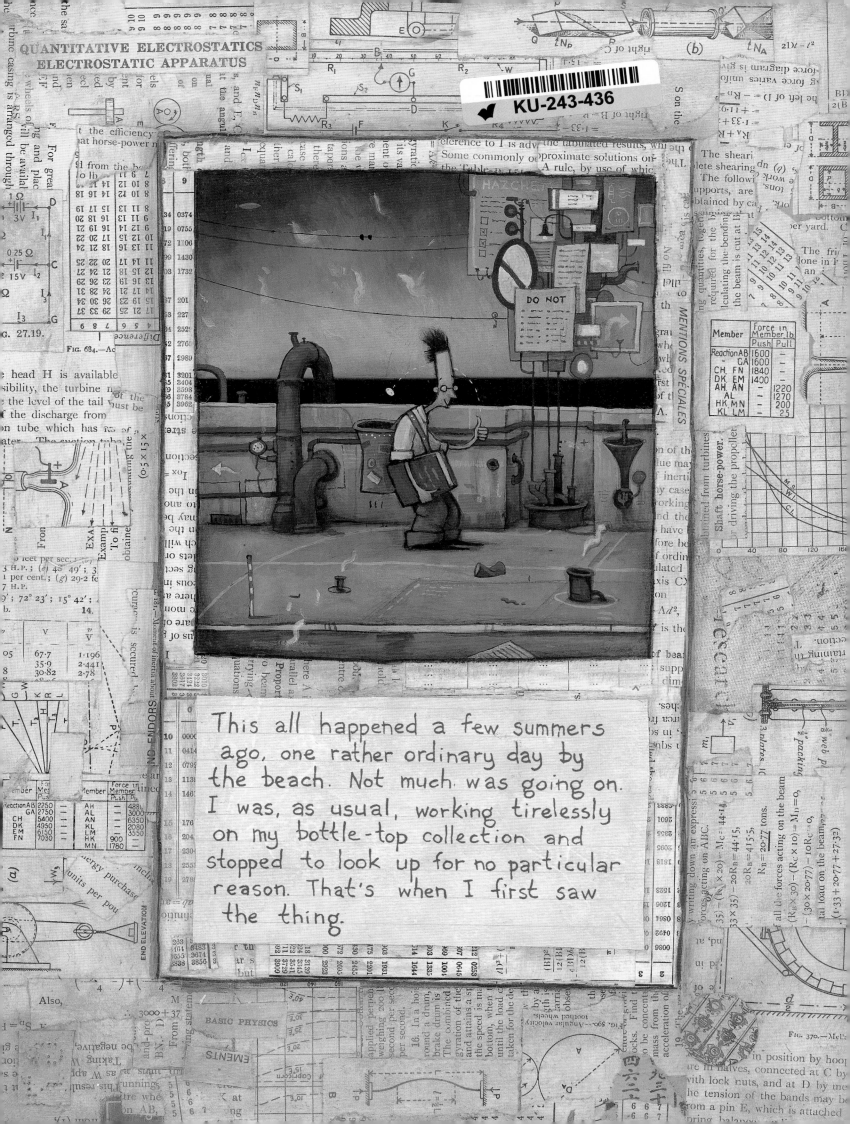

This all happened a few summers ago, one rather ordinary day by the beach. Not much was going on. I was, as usual, working tirelessly on my bottle-top collection and stopped to look up for no particular reason. That's when I first saw the thing.

I must have stared at it for a while. I mean, it had
a really weird look about it — a sad, lost sort of look.
Nobody else seemed to notice it was there.
Too busy doing beach stuff, I guess.

Naturally, I was intrigued. I decided to investigate.

sure didn't do much.

It just sat there,

looking out of place.

I was baffled.

It was quite friendly though, once I started talking to it.

ANTI-LOGARITHMS

I played with the thing for most of the afternoon. It was great fun, yet I couldn't help feeling that something wasn't quite right.

Exercise 7*b**

As the hours slouched by, it seemed less and less likely that anybody was coming to take the thing home. There was no denying the unhappy truth of the situation It was <u>lost</u>.

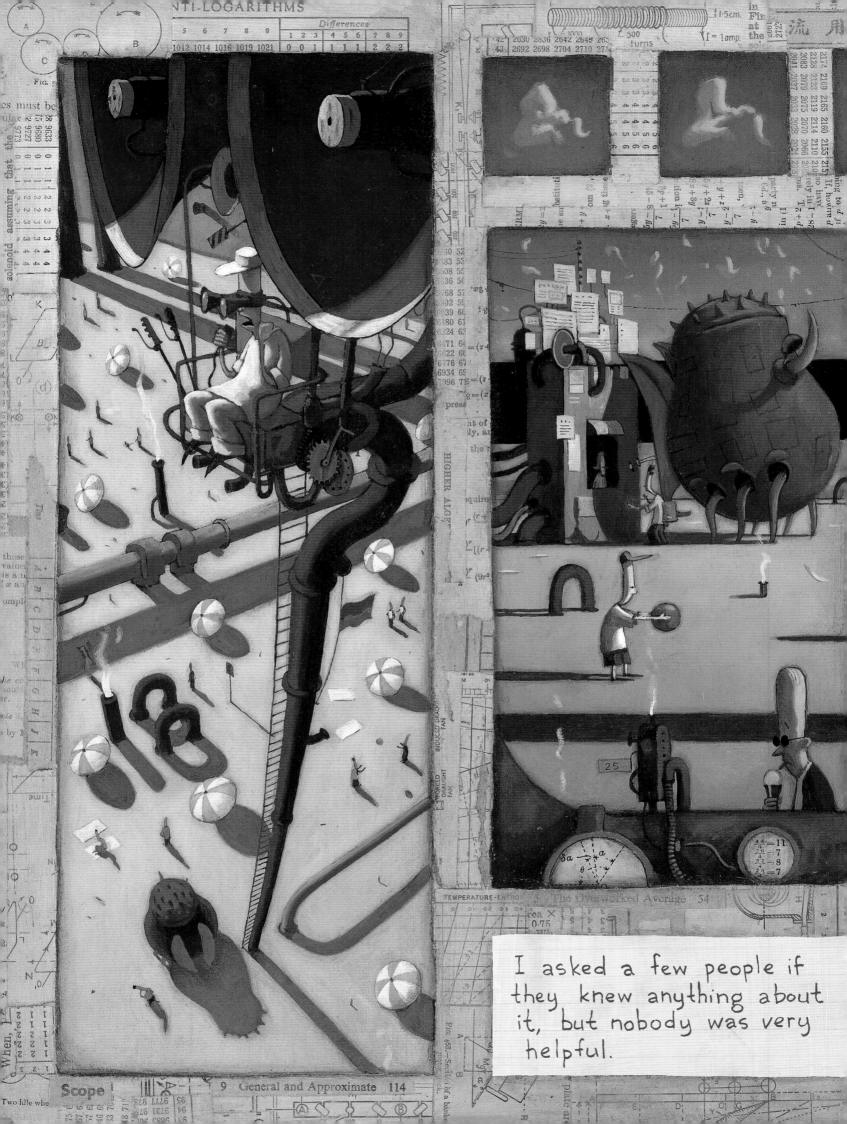

I asked a few people if they knew anything about it, but nobody was very helpful.

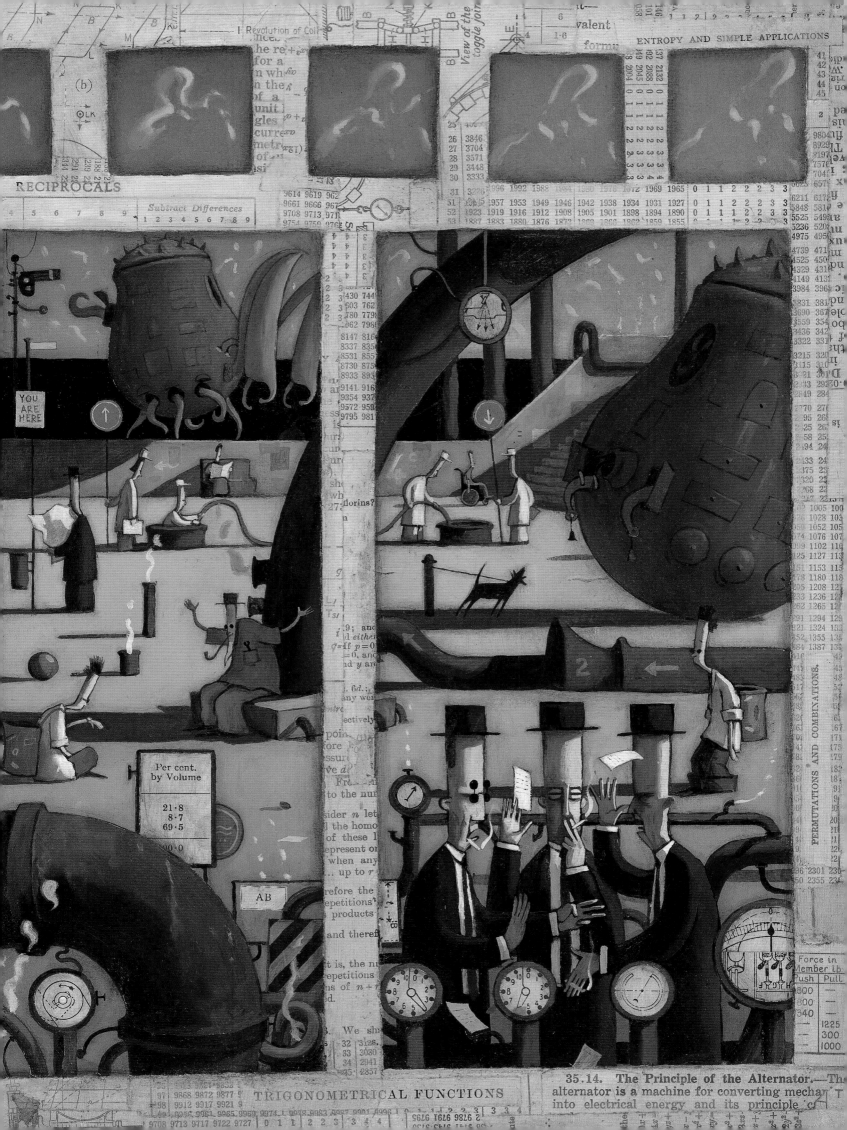

I took the lost thing over to Pete's place. Pete has an opinion on just about everything.

'Cool,' he said.

'I'm trying to find out who owns it,' I told him.
'I dunno, man,' said Pete. 'It's pretty weird. Maybe it doesn't belong to anyone. Maybe it doesn't come from anywhere. Some things are like that...'
He paused for dramatic effect, '...just plain lost.'

2   Scope   18

3   Seeing Things   28

4   Reality   43

There was nothing left to do but take the thing home with me. I mean, I couldn't just leave it wandering the streets. Plus I felt kind of sorry for it.

My parents didn't really notice it at first.
Too busy discussing current events, I guess.

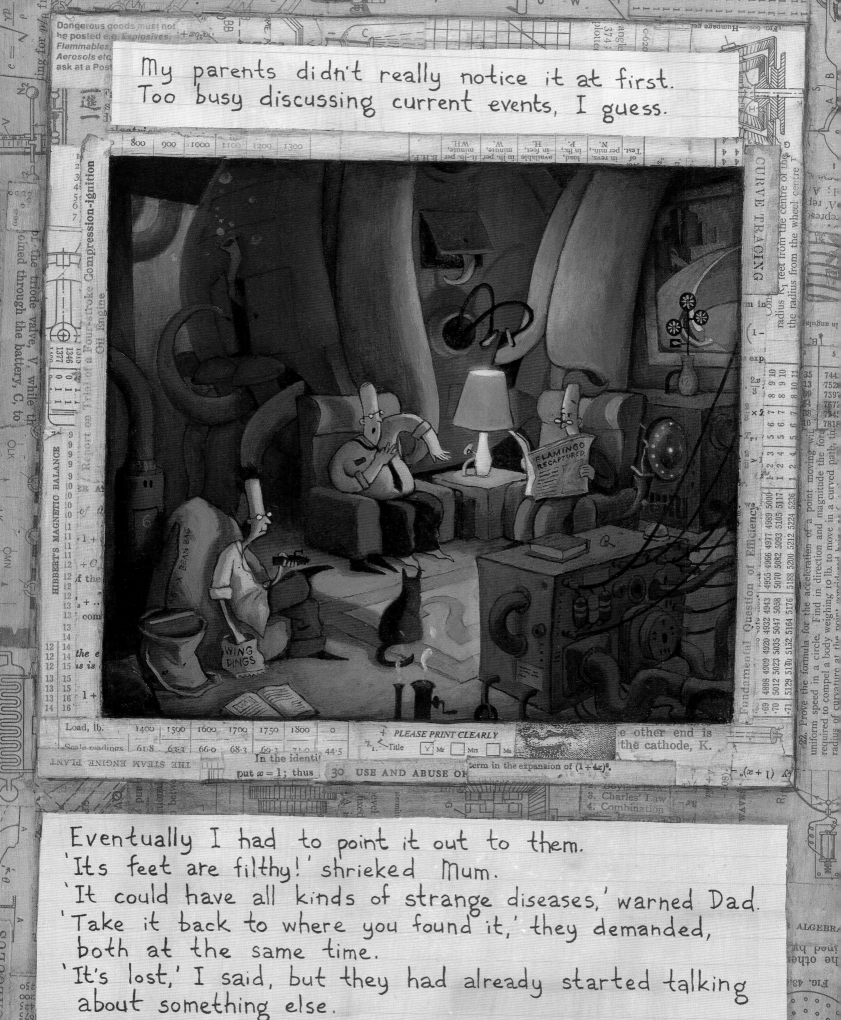

Eventually I had to point it out to them.
'Its feet are filthy!' shrieked Mum.
'It could have all kinds of strange diseases,' warned Dad.
'Take it back to where you found it,' they demanded,
both at the same time.
'It's lost,' I said, but they had already started talking
about something else.

I hid the thing in our back shed and gave it something to eat, once I found out what it liked. It seemed a bit happier then, even though it was still lost.

I checked the local paper for any lost pet notices, but only found a lot of good deals on refrigerator repairs. I remember thinking then that Pete was probably right, that some things were just plain lost. In any case, I sure couldn't keep the thing in the shed forever. Mum or Dad would eventually notice it when they came out looking for a hammer or something.

It was a real dilemma.

I was wondering what to do when a small advertisement on the last page of the paper happened to catch my eye.

bureaucritae opacus.

0.2676	1.7968
0.2762	1.7884
0.2836	1.7884
0.2006	1.7807

THE FEDERAL DEPARTMENT OF ECONOMICS

consumere ergo sum.

We understand that at the end of the d all that matters is the balance sheet.

YOU
ARE YOU FINDING THAT THE ORDER OF DAY-TO-DAY LIFE IS UNEXPECTEDLY DISRUPTED BY

UNCLAIMED PROPERTY?

OBJECTS WITHOUT NAMES?

TROUBLESOME ARTIFACTS OF UNKNOWN ORIGIN?

FILING CABINET LEFTOVERS?

THINGS THAT JUST DON'T BELONG?

DON'T PANIC!

We've got a pigeon hole to stick it in.

Community Service Announcement

...NOW YOUR DIODES

A21/B A21/C ZX40

UXB42 DDU98 Zx(a)

...F5(a) TYX23 HU84-C GL56

THE FEDERAL DEPARTMENT OF ODDS & ENDS

sweepus underum carpetae.

Downtown,
6328th Street
Tall Grey Building #357b

...PARTMENT OF TUBES & PIPES

plumbiferus ductus.

The next morning we caught a tram into the city.

We arrived at a tall grey building with no windows. It was pretty dark in there, and it smelt like disinfectant. 'I have a lost thing,' I called to the receptionist at the front desk.
'Fill in these forms,' she said.

The lost thing made a small, sad noise.

I was looking around for a pen when I felt something tug the back of my shirt.
'If you really care about that thing, you shouldn't leave it here,' said a tiny voice. 'This is a place for forgetting, leaving behind, smoothing over. Here, take this.'

It was a business card with a kind of sign on it. It wasn't very important looking, but it did seem to point somewhere. 'Cheers,' I said.

Eventually we found what seemed to be the right place, in a dark little gap off some anonymous little street. The sort of place you'd never know existed unless you were actually looking for it.

I pressed a buzzer on the wall and this big door opened up.

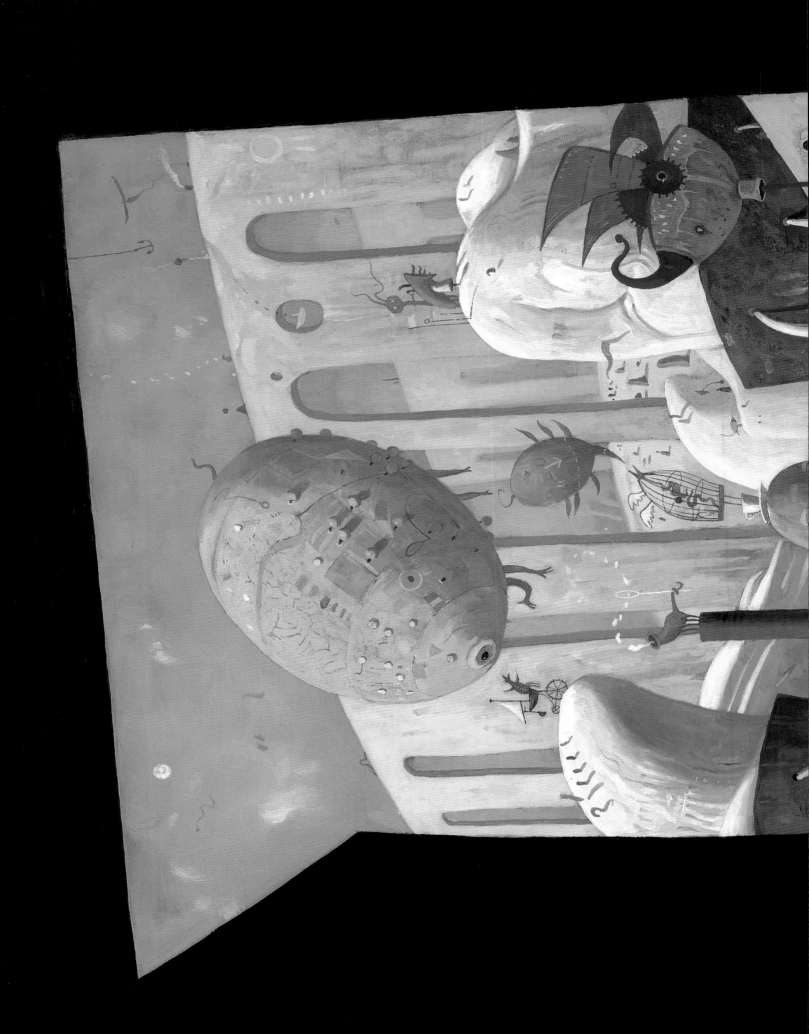

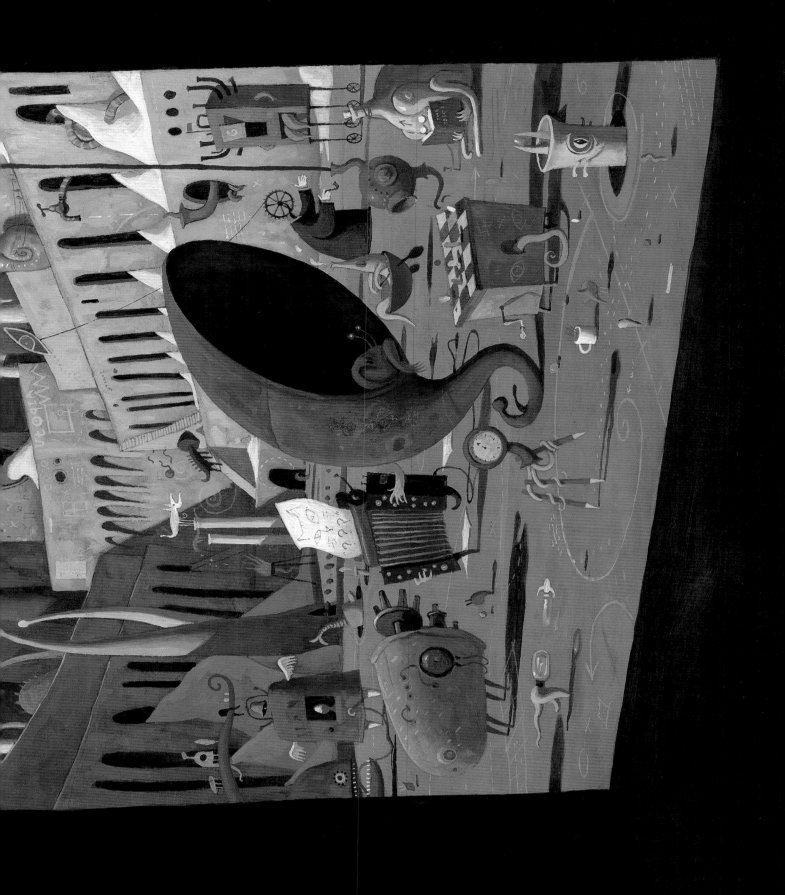

I didn't know what to think, but the lost thing made an approving sort of noise. It seemed as good a time as any to say goodbye to each other. So we did.

Then I went home to classify my bottle-top collection.

Well, that's it. That's the story.
Not especially profound, I know, but I never said it was.
And don't ask me what the moral is.

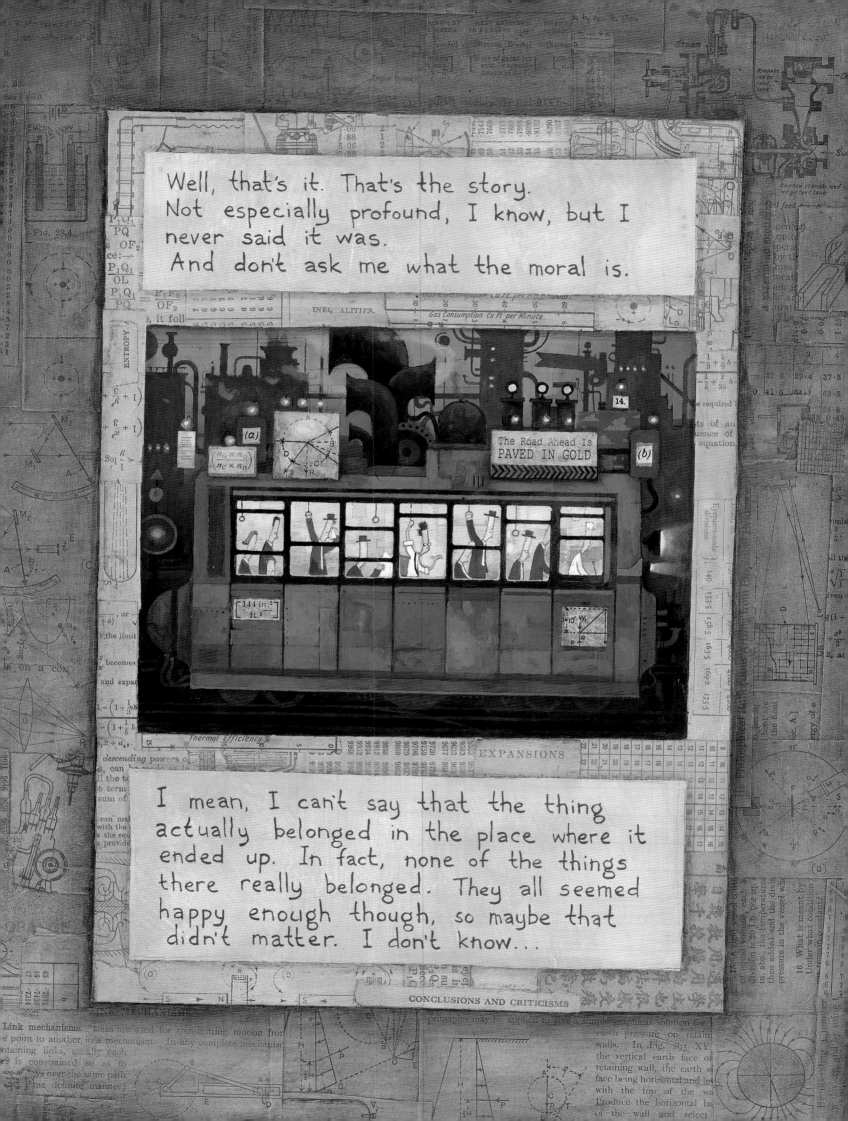

I mean, I can't say that the thing actually belonged in the place where it ended up. In fact, none of the things there really belonged. They all seemed happy enough though, so maybe that didn't matter. I don't know...

I still think about that lost thing from time to time. Especially when I see something out of the corner of my eye that doesn't quite fit.

You know, something with a weird, sad, lost sort of look.

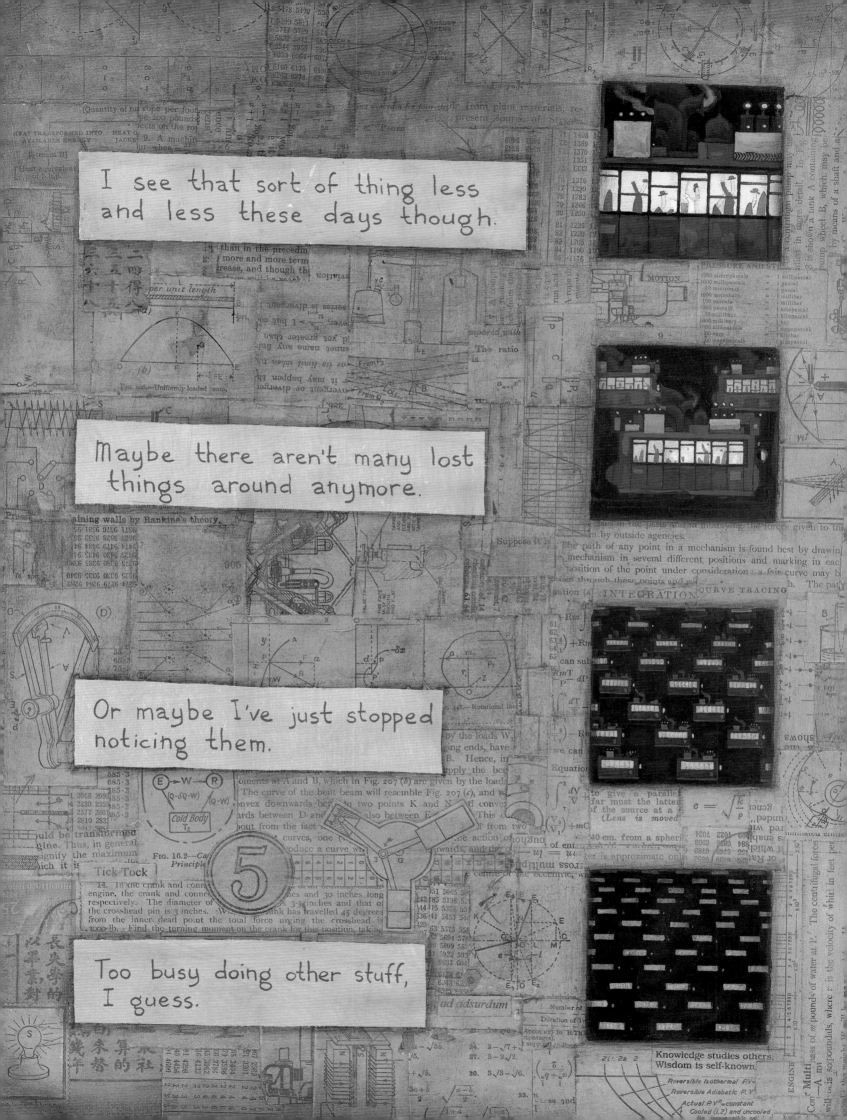

I see that sort of thing less and less these days though.

Maybe there aren't many lost things around anymore.

Or maybe I've just stopped noticing them.

Too busy doing other stuff, I guess.

And APOLOGIES to Edward Hopper / Jeffrey Smart, John Brack

Gary Crew

The Funkmeister

Paul & The Twins

BILL DAY

the freo centre folk,

lit

and for valued interest and comments from
Jonathan, Keira, Robin,

with THANKS to Helen Chamberlin   Chris D. a fellow connoisseur of
heavy duty industrial plumbing

Editorial technician #264